NEPTUNE ADVENTURES

#1 DANGER ON CRAB ISLAND

Avon Books are available at special quantity discounts for bulk purchases for sales promotions, premiums, fund raising or educational use. Special books, or book excerpts, can also be created to fit specific needs.

For details write or telephone the office of the Director of Special Markets, Avon Books, Inc., Dept. FP, 1350 Avenue of the Americas, New York, New York 10019, 1-800-238-0658.

NEPTUNE ADVENTURES

#1 DANGER ON CRAB ISLAND

SUSAN SAUNDERS

AN AVON CAMELOT BOOK

This is a work of fiction. Names, characters, places, and incidents either are the product of the author's imagination or are used fictitiously. Any resemblance to actual events, locales, organizations, or persons, living or dead, is entirely coincidental and beyond the intent of either the author or the publisher.

AVON BOOKS, INC.
1350 Avenue of the Americas
New York, New York 10019

Copyright © 1998 by Susan Saunders
Published by arrangement with the author
Visit our website at http://www.AvonBooks.com
Library of Congress Catalog Card Number: 97-94283
ISBN: 0-380-79488-8

First Avon Camelot Printing: April 1998

CAMELOT TRADEMARK REG. U.S. PAT. OFF. AND IN OTHER COUNTRIES, MARCA REGISTRADA, HECHO EN U.S.A.

Printed in the U.S.A.

OPM 10 9 8 7 6 5 4

To Artemis Millan, my kayaking partner

NEPTUNE ADVENTURES

#1 DANGER ON CRAB ISLAND

CHAPTER ONE

"Hey, Mom!" Dana Chapin called out. "I could use some more squid over here!"

It was an icy winter Sunday, and Dana was working at one end of the Project Neptune food-prep shed, practically up to her nose in raw fish. Pieces of flounder, herring, and cod—eyeballs, tails, and all—were piled on the steel table in front of her.

At the other end of the shed, Mrs. Chapin was chopping up whole fish and squid into chunks that seals could swallow.

Dana filled plastic bags and buckets with the cold, slimy stuff. The bags would go into the giant freezer. Then Dana and her mom would carry the buckets into the stranding barn, where the seal cages were. It was just a small part of the work to be done at Project Neptune.

The Chapins' Project Neptune rescued sick and stranded sea creatures like seals, dolphins, and turtles. Once they'd even saved a young whale that had washed up on a beach miles away. Dana's mom and dad had started the Project twelve years earlier, right before Dana was born.

Joe and Lissa Chapin were both marine biologists. They were teaching at a city university when they read a story in the newspaper about a lighthouse for sale—Parsons Point Light, it was called.

The Chapins had visited the place and loved it. The two-hundred-year-old lighthouse was perched on the edge of a rocky cliff that jutted into the Atlantic Ocean. It stood beside the migration routes of seals, sea turtles, and many different kinds of birds.

That first day, Dana's father had spotted a humpback whale from the tower, diving for food in the cold Atlantic. Dana's mother had discovered a harbor seal colony hauled out on a narrow beach at the bottom of the cliff.

There was a stone house attached to the tower, where the Chapins could live. There were also three large wooden outbuildings on the Point, which could be hooked together into one huge stranding barn that would eventually hold cages and exercise tanks for rescued sea animals.

There were drawbacks, of course. No one had lived at Parsons Point for fifty years or more; all of the buildings needed major repairs. But Dana's parents had used their savings to buy Parsons Point because it seemed perfect for what they wanted to do: rescue stranded sea animals, nurse them back to health, and return them to the Atlantic Ocean when they were strong again.

At the very beginning the Neptune staff was just Joe and Lissa Chapin. Dr. Martin Bucalo was their part-time veterinarian.

Then Dr. Bucalo had joined Neptune full time. So had Carol Prentice, a bookkeeper, and Walter McGrath, who edited *Neptune Adventures*, the monthly newsletter. Walter also put together video programs about Neptune's work.

But Project Neptune couldn't have functioned without its volunteers. Neptuners, they called themselves, and there were more than a hundred and fifty of them. The youngest was Bobby Durham, who was eight years old. The oldest was Mr. Garber, who was eighty-three.

Neptuners patrolled the coastline in all kinds of weather. They cleaned up the beaches to keep seabirds and animals from eating garbage or getting caught in it. They gathered information on local seals and whales, and searched for stranded seals, dolphins, and turtles. Some Neptuners looked after the animals recovering at Parsons Point.

Dana had helped out at Neptune since she was big enough to carry things. "And having Tyler here will give us another set of hands," she thought out loud as she filled a fifth bucket with fish.

Tyler was Dana's first cousin, her Uncle Jim's son. He and Dana were practically the same age; their birthdays were just ten days apart. Dana had only seen her cousin a few times in her entire life, though. Her dad's brother Jim and his wife had moved to Alaska before Tyler was born.

Uncle Jim was a biologist, too, but he worked on land, and he'd just gotten a grant to study wolves in the Arctic for a year. Since Tyler's mom had died when he was a baby, Tyler was coming to live with Dana's family at Parsons Point until Uncle Jim finished the study.

There was plenty of room for a guest at the lighthouse. Dana had helped her dad repaint one of their spare bedrooms a deep blue-green for Tyler. But Dana wasn't sure how much she was going to like having another kid around all the time, especially somebody she didn't really know.

Dana had last seen Tyler in California five years earlier. Her parents had gone to a Marine Mammals Conference in San Francisco, and they'd taken Dana along. Uncle Jim and Tyler had flown down from Fairbanks for a visit. Only seven then, Tyler was small for his age. And as Dana remembered it, he didn't have much to say to her.

"Dana?"

Her mom's voice made Dana jump.

"Why are you looking so serious?" Mrs. Chapin said to her daughter. She dumped a mound of squid on the table in front of Dana and started scooping it up by the handful, adding it to the buckets of fish.

Mrs. Chapin and Dana both wore rubber gloves—not to keep the fishy smells off their hands, but to keep human smells off the seals' food.

"Too early in the day to get up close and personal with fish heads?" Mrs. Chapin said.

"Uh-huh." Dana didn't want to admit that she was worrying about Tyler.

"Your dad and Tyler should be back from the airport soon," said her mother, who sometimes seemed to be able to read Dana's mind. "Let's get those seals fed." Mrs. Chapin added vitamin pellets to each of the six buckets of fish. "Chow time."

Dana and her mom slipped into their jackets. Mrs. Chapin picked up three of the buckets and Dana picked up three more.

The food-prep shed leaned against a side of the huge

4

stranding barn. Dana slid open the door between them with one rubber-booted foot, and she and her mom stepped into the barn.

The stranding barn wasn't heated. The seals at Neptune were not pets; they were wild animals, and the Chapins wanted them to stay that way. So the air inside the barn was almost as cold as it was on the winter beaches outside. Dana's breath made little white clouds in the air.

Right now there were six seals being cared for by Project Neptune: five harbor seals and a grey seal. The harbor seals had short brownish gray fur speckled with darker spots. They had stiff white whiskers and eyebrows, and smooth, round heads with no outer ears, just earholes. Their large brown eyes were intelligent and curious. They looked like big, slick dogs.

But Dana was careful to stare at the buckets and not at the seals as she dumped fish, squid, and vitamins into the first two cages. Neither Dana nor her mom touched the seals while they were feeding them. They never spoke to the animals. If they had to talk to each other, they whispered. They never looked into the seals' eyes.

Getting used to humans would do the animals much more harm than good when they were returned to the ocean. Sometimes it was really hard for Dana, though, because they were so cute!

The seals in the first two cages were named Harold and Maude. Both had been brought to Neptune in November, thin and weak. Harold had had pneumonia. Maude had become so tangled up in a piece of fish net that she'd almost starved to death.

But after a month and a half with plenty to eat, plus vitamins and medicine, they were well on their way

5

to a full recovery. They'd probably be released in a few weeks.

Ellie, the little grey seal, wasn't so lucky. She was named for Dr. Bucalo's wife, Eleanor. The Bucalos' son, Luke, had found Ellie washed up on a beach not far from Parsons Point with an eye infection. She'd recovered from the infection, but she'd been left almost totally blind.

Grey seals normally travel thousands of miles in their yearly migrations, but Ellie couldn't manage the long trip without her eyesight. The Chapins would eventually have to find a permanent home for her at a zoo or aquarium.

Since Ellie would be dealing with humans for the rest of her life, Dana's mom and dad said she might as well get used to them at Neptune. And the little seal was becoming really tame. She could recognize Dana's smell fifty feet away.

Ellie wriggled excitedly while Dana rubbed her head through the bars of the cage. She gobbled down her raw fish and squid in a few seconds. Then Dana opened the door to her cage so that she could spend some time swimming in a tank, strengthening her muscles.

With Dana's help, Ellie swayed down the gangplank and dived into the water. Her long, stiff whiskers brushed against the sides of the tank, guiding her as she glided around and around. Every few minutes, Ellie surfaced with a loud *whuff*, took a breath, then jackknifed down again.

Dana was still watching the seal breeze around the tank when the barn door slid open.

"Well, here we are!" Dana's dad announced in a loud whisper. He was all smiles.

The boy behind him didn't seem nearly so happy.

He was a head taller than Dana, and skinny, with

6

curly brown hair. He'd have been okay-looking if he hadn't had such a miserable expression on his face.

"Dana, say hi to your cousin," Mr. Chapin whispered.

Dana gave it her best shot. "Hi!" she whispered to Tyler. "Come meet Ellie."

"Maybe later," Tyler mumbled, barely glancing at the tank, or at any of the other animals, either. "Uncle Joe, can I see my room?" And he stepped back through the door.

Wow! How could anybody resist seals? Most visitors fell in love with them at first sight! Already Dana had a strong feeling that Tyler wasn't going to be the help she'd hoped for around Neptune.

"Excellent meeting you, too," someone murmured in Dana's ear.

It was Luke Bucalo. He and his folks lived right down the road, and since Dr. Bucalo spent a lot of time at Neptune, Luke was often there, too—when he wasn't playing baseball or soccer or practicing for high school swimming meets.

Luke was sort of like Dana's big brother. Sometimes they went kayaking or hiking together. And he was teaching Dana to rock climb on the cliffs below the lighthouse.

Luke grinned down at her. "Real friendly," he said about Tyler.

"Bummer," Dana said with a sigh.

Mrs. Chapin was waving to Dana from the doorway. "Let's go over to the house," she mouthed to her daughter.

"I'll keep an eye on Ellie," Luke whispered to Dana.

Dana nodded. She took a last deep breath of the cold, fishy air and headed for the door.

7

CHAPTER TWO

This was probably the worst day of Tyler Chapin's life. Okay, maybe it was the *second* worst day.

The worst day was when his dad had told him that he'd be living in the Canadian Arctic for the year. For a few seconds, Tyler had imagined himself camping out in the wilderness with his father, surrounded by snow and ice and wolves, like real frontiersmen! Then Tyler's dad had burst his bubble. He'd announced that Tyler would be spending the year with his uncle and aunt and cousin in the Lower Forty-eight.

Now his home in Alaska was several thousand miles away. He'd left Thane, his malamute, and all of his friends behind. He didn't know anyone here. Life as Tyler knew it would be on hold for twelve months. In a weird way, the only thing that kind of cheered him up was that his cousin Dana didn't seem any happier about the arrangement than he was.

"Misery loves company," Mrs. Watkins, his next-door neighbor, would have said. Mrs. Watkins was taking care of Thane for him.

Tyler followed his uncle out of the barn, through the small, heated lean-to where the animals' food was prepared, to the outside.

"No mountains?" Tyler asked his uncle, although he already knew the answer just from glancing around.

"Not for several hundred miles," his uncle said.

Where Tyler lived, near Fairbanks, there were mountain peaks and clear blue sky in all directions.

Here, everything was flat and gray. Gray land, gray water . . . gray sky. The air was heavy and damp, not sharp and dry like it was in Alaska in the wintertime. And where was the snow?

Tyler and his uncle walked past a square brick building.

"The veterinary clinic's in there, and the Neptune office," Mr. Chapin told his nephew.

Tyler nodded, but he wasn't really listening. He was still thinking about his log house in Alaska, with the snow-covered White Mountains towering over it.

Uncle Joe lifted Tyler's suitcases out of the dark blue Project Neptune pickup. Then he opened the back door of the house below the tower. "We're home!" he said to Tyler.

Maybe you are, Tyler said to himself. *But I'm not!* He wouldn't have thought it was possible to feel so crummy.

A black woodstove simmered in a corner of an old-fashioned kitchen. A big yellow dog was lying on the floor next to the stove. He scrambled to his feet. First he jumped all over Uncle Joe, then he tried to lick Tyler's face.

"This is Jake," said Uncle Joe.

"Hey, Jake," Tyler said, patting the dog and missing Thane more than ever.

"Your bedroom is right down this hall," his uncle said. He stepped back and let Tyler walk into the room first.

Tyler could smell fresh paint, so he said, "Nice color," and managed a weak smile.

"Glad you like it," said his uncle. "Your cousin Dana and I painted it last weekend."

Uncle Joe set Tyler's suitcases down in the middle of the plank floor. "Your bed's made, there are extra blankets in the closet, the chest of drawers is empty . . . and that's Badger Bay out the window. Those low buildings on the far side of the bay are the wharves in downtown Rockport. Your school is just beyond them."

"Mmm-hmm," said Tyler, not even wanting to *think* about starting a new school. "Is it okay if I unpack my stuff?"

"Sure," Mr. Chapin answered. "I can hear your aunt and Dana stirring around in the kitchen. I'll call you when we've gotten some food on the table."

"Great," said Tyler.

As soon as his uncle started down the hall, Tyler closed the door to the bedroom. He unzipped his backpack, took out a picture of Thane, with Sawtooth Mountain in the background, and set it on the chest of drawers. Next to it he placed a photo of his dad with a gray wolf.

Then Tyler pulled out a brand-new calendar and a marker. He opened the calendar to January and made a big X across the square that read, "Sunday, January 17."

"One down, almost. Three hundred sixty-four to go,"

10

he murmured to himself. How was he going to get through 364 more days of *this*?

"Tyler, lunch is ready," his aunt called from the kitchen.

"Coming," Tyler said.

He stuck the calendar on a hook in the closet and headed up the hall.

His aunt and uncle were good cooks, at least. Aunt Lissa had roasted a turkey—Tyler got a drumstick. And Uncle Joe had made sweet potatoes and cornbread stuffing.

But Tyler learned right away that meals at the Chapins' house were often interrupted. The four of them had barely started eating when a black wall phone rang in the kitchen.

"I'll get it," Uncle Joe said quickly, pushing his chair back.

"That's the stranding phone," Aunt Lissa told Tyler. "It's a separate number."

" 'Stranding'?" Tyler said, not understanding.

"It means an animal has washed up on a beach and it's too sick or hurt to swim away again," Dana explained.

"What species?" Uncle Joe was saying into the phone. "Harbor? . . . A hooded seal! We haven't had a hooded this winter. . . . How does it look? . . . Young . . . Okay, you know what to do. We'll get there as fast as we can."

Uncle Joe hung up the phone. "A young hooded seal stranded on Indian Beach. Mr. Garber found him—says he's very weak," he said. "Dana, call Martin. Tell him your mom and I have to load some things in the truck, and that we'll pick him up on our way past his house."

11

"Can't I go with you?" Dana said.

"No, you stay here with your cousin," said Uncle Joe.

"But—" Dana began.

"Dana—" said Aunt Lissa.

"Oh, all right," Dana mumbled.

"I'll be okay by myself," Tyler said quickly. In fact, he'd welcome some time alone.

Tyler was the only kid in his house in Alaska. He was sometimes the only *person* because his dad's schedule was never the same from one day to the next. Jim Chapin might be giving a talk to graduate students at the college, monitoring Alaskan wolf packs, or serving as an adviser at the zoo.

He always left plenty of food in the freezer for his son, in case he didn't make it home in time for dinner himself. On those evenings, Tyler nuked something in the microwave and shared his meal with Thane.

Jake was lying across Tyler's hiking boots under the table, and Tyler was sure the yellow dog would appreciate a slice of turkey.

But Aunt Lissa said, "I want the two of you to finish your lunch, and then maybe you'd like to take a nap, Tyler. You've just traveled halfway around the world."

Without waiting for a reply, Aunt Lissa pulled on her rubber boots again, grabbed her jacket, and hurried out to help Uncle Joe. He was already outside, carrying blankets and pads out of the barn and dumping them in the back of the pickup truck.

Dana picked up a phone in the hall and punched in the Bucalos' number.

"Mrs. Bucalo? Hi," Dana said. "There's a hooded

seal stranded on Indian Beach. . . . Mom and Dad will pick Doc up in a few minutes, okay? . . . Thanks.''

She walked slowly back to the kitchen table and sat down again.

"What good does saving one seal do?'' Tyler asked her. "Seals get killed all the time. And there are probably hundreds of thousands of them in the world, anyway.'' *Not like wolves*, he almost added.

Dana frowned at him. "Hooded seals happen to be really rare here. After all, they're Arctic seals,'' she said. "Besides, saving seals and dolphins and turtles is a great way to get people to think about the environment, and about what they can do to make it better.''

"Okay, okay,'' Tyler said, holding up his hands.

"I'm finished eating,'' Dana said, still frowning. She carried her plate to the sink. "I'm going up in the tower.''

"I'll come, too,'' said Tyler. He'd never been to the top of a lighthouse.

The cousins entered the tower through a low door in the dining-room wall and started climbing toward the giant light. The wrought iron steps curved around and around, narrowing as the tower narrowed.

The stone walls held in the cold. By the time Dana and Tyler reached the tiny platform at the top of the tower, they were panting. But they were also shivering from the damp chill.

The light itself was made of squares of thick, heavy glass. In the center of the squares, a lens sparkled like a giant jewel.

"Does this thing work?'' Tyler asked his cousin.

Dana shrugged. "Probably,'' she replied. "Dad says the lenses in some of these old lights are so good that

13

the flame in a small oil lamp could be seen twenty-five miles out to sea. But we've never lit it. It might confuse fishermen, since they're looking for the light at the Coast Guard station.''

Dana gazed out the windows toward the open ocean. "I love this view," she murmured.

Tyler didn't say anything. From the tower, everything seemed even flatter and grayer to him.

Then he noticed something interesting. "Whose kayaks?" he asked, pointing down at two brightly colored kayaks beside a boat dock on the bay side.

"The purple one's mine, and the yellow one's Luke's," Dana said.

"Cool," said Tyler. "I'd like to try one out."

"Have you ever kayaked?" Dana wanted to know.

"No, but I've canoed, and I know that's a lot harder," Tyler said carelessly. "I could explore in a kayak—like check out that little island over there." He meant a string of large boulders where the mouth of Badger Bay opened into the Atlantic Ocean.

"No, you can't," Dana said firmly. "That's Crab Island, and I've never even been there myself. It's too dangerous. If the wind is blowing from the northeast, giant waves can crash all the way across those rocks."

Giant waves? Tyler said to himself, gazing down at the bay. *Give me a break. It's as calm as a pond.*

Aloud, he said, "So I won't go when the wind blows from the northeast."

"You won't go at all," Dana told him. "Dad won't let me kayak alone, and you can't either. And we sure won't be paddling across the bay. The currents are really strong. Plus we might get run over by a fishing boat."

"How likely is that?" Tyler muttered, since there

wasn't a boat in sight. He was beginning to realize there were a lot of rules for the Parsons Point Chapins, rules that he wasn't necessarily going to agree with.

"Right now, I'd like to go to my room—if you think that would be okay," Tyler added with his eyebrows raised.

He started down the iron steps of the tower, but he could hear Dana mumbling something above him.

"What did you say?" Tyler asked her, feeling ornery.

"I said I'm going out to the stranding barn to help Luke," Dana told him.

That was all right with Tyler. Suddenly he'd never felt so tired in his life. He made it down the lighthouse stairs, then stumbled through the dining room and along the hall with Jake tagging behind him.

Tyler dragged a wool blanket out of the closet in his room. He collapsed onto the bed without even kicking off his hiking boots.

As he pulled the blanket up over his shoulders, he felt Jake jump onto the bed and ease up beside him.

A second later, Tyler fell into a deep sleep.

CHAPTER THREE

It felt weird for Dana to be showing up at Rockport Middle School on Monday with an unknown cousin. And she was certain it was hard for Tyler, too: He was the only new kid in seventh grade, when almost everyone else had known each other forever.

At lunch in the cafeteria that first day, Dana introduced Tyler around. He met Dana's best friend, Kim Meyers, and Cassie Parker and Jason Booth and Andrew Reed, some of the other kids she hung out with. Kim, Andrew, and Jason were volunteers at Neptune, too.

But instead of trying to fit in, Tyler seemed to go out of his way to make things more difficult. At first he didn't bother to join in the conversation. Cassie and Andrew were cousins, and they were excited about a cross-country ski vacation their parents were planning for spring break.

"Is there much cross-country skiing where you live in Alaska?" Kim asked Tyler, just to include him.

Tyler shrugged his shoulders, and said, "Alaska's got

16

major peaks—it's not flat like it is down here. Anybody over five years old skis downhill.''

"I skied downhill at Sugarbush, in Vermont," Jason said. "We had to wait forever for the lifts."

"In Alaska we don't have to stand in line for anything," Tyler said. "It's more like the Wild West."

Dana caught Cassie and Jason making faces, and Andrew left the table as soon as he'd gulped down a chili dog. He said he had to check a book out of the library.

Kim was nice about Tyler, though. "He's not really bragging; he's just uncomfortable, being the new kid in town," she said to Dana when lunch was over. "He'll settle down in a few days."

"Maybe . . . ," Dana said. But she wasn't so sure.

She was relieved that she and Tyler didn't have any classes together. She'd have been so uneasy about what he might say or do that she couldn't possibly have paid any attention to her teachers.

On Tuesday Tyler slouched over to a corner of the cafeteria to eat lunch by himself, and Dana was glad. Just because her cousin insisted on making himself unpopular didn't mean she wanted to go down the tubes with him.

When school was over that afternoon, Dana hurried out to the parking lot to get on the bus. Tyler was already standing near the curb—and he was joking around with Charlie and Carter, the Mote twins!

He couldn't have picked anybody worse to hang out with if he'd tried. Some of the kids called Charlie Mote "Mote-orino," because he never stopped his motor-mouthing—especially during class. He was always in trouble, either for talking too much or for doing goofy stuff like falling out of his chair on purpose.

17

Carter Mote hardly ever talked. He also never combed his hair. Or brushed his teeth.

Dana's parents said it was because the twins' mother didn't live with them, their dad worked long hours, and there was no one really taking care of them. Whatever the reason, the twins looked totally grubby most of the time. Plus they got terrible grades.

But there was more to it than that between the Motes and the Chapins. Dana's mom and dad had had problems with the twins' father, Wilbur Mote.

Mr. Mote was a commercial fisherman who hated everything about Project Neptune. He thought conservationists just enjoyed interfering with fishermen making an honest living.

A few months before, Mr. Mote and a few others had aired their complaints about Neptune on *Viewpoint,* a program on WLIR, the Rockport television channel.

"Meddlesome city folks, that's all they are, coming in here to mess up our lives! They try to tell us *when* to fish, *what* to fish, *how* to fish, when they don't know the first thing about it themselves! Change our nets so we don't snag any seals?" Mr. Mote had thundered. "Why should we worry about the blasted seals? Our catches are half the size they used to be. And it's no wonder, with twice as many seals eating everything that swims in the sea!"

Then Mr. and Mrs. Chapin had taken their turn on TV. It wasn't the seals that were causing smaller catches—it was years and years of overfishing, Dana's dad explained. Mrs. Chapin added that seals don't even eat many of the kinds of fish that humans eat.

They showed photographs of seals and dolphins tangled in nets or dead from having swallowed large fishhooks, and they talked about how sea animals were important to the food chain.

Dana thought her folks had made a lot of sense on *Viewpoint*. Other people must have thought so, too: The Chapins' television appearance brought even more volunteers to Project Neptune.

But the Chapins certainly hadn't changed Mr. Mote's mind. If anything, he seemed even angrier. Whenever he spotted Dana and her parents in Rockport, Mr. Mote gave them dirty looks and muttered under his breath.

And here Tyler was, making friends with the Mote twins—when they were practically the enemy!

Dana walked up behind her cousin and gave him a nudge.

"What?" Tyler said over his shoulder.

"I need to talk to you," Dana said, cutting her eyes at Charlie and Carter. "In private."

Tyler shrugged. "Catch you later," he said to the Motes.

"Later, dude!" Charlie said.

Carter just nodded.

Dana climbed onto the school bus and slid into an empty seat.

Tyler sank down on the seat next to her. "So?" he said.

"Hanging around with the Motes is a bad idea. They're always in trouble at school. And they don't get along with my family," Dana told Tyler.

"Why not?" he asked her, surprised.

"Because of Project Neptune," Dana said. "Mr. Mote hates Project Neptune."

"Well, that's nothing to do with me," Tyler said shortly. He stood up and walked to the back of the bus.

19

Dana saw him waving to Charlie and Carter through the window as the bus rolled out of the parking lot.

After a half-dozen stops, the school bus pulled onto the shoulder of Harbor Lane, opposite the gravel road that cut across the Point to the lighthouse. Dana waited for Tyler to get off the bus before she started for home. But as soon as Tyler's sneakers hit the ground, he said, "Go on without me. I want to take a closer look at those kayaks."

"Okay," Dana said. "But you know you can't—"

"Yeah, yeah," Tyler said, "I know what I *can't* do. You tell me every couple of seconds!" He stamped away, headed for the rocky bank above the bay beach.

Dana was about to go into the house when she remembered the young hooded seal her folks had brought in the day before, so she walked over to the clinic instead.

Dr. Bucalo was sitting at his desk, tapping the keys of a computer.

"Hi! How's the new little seal doing?" Dana asked him.

"Hold on—I'm just finishing my report for the East Coast Stranding Network," Dr. Bucalo said. He finished tapping, hit the ENTER key, and stood up. "Want to take a look at him? He's sleeping."

As he opened the door to the infirmary, Dr. Bucalo said in a low voice, "He'll stay in here where it's warm until he's a lot stronger."

"He's beautiful," Dana whispered, peering into the big cage where the hooded seal lay on his side.

He was less than a year old, but much larger than harbor seals the same age. He was also a different color. His thick coat was blue-gray along his back and silvery

20

on the underside. A rectangular patch of fur had been shaved off the seal's stomach. Dana could see a long incision there, with lots of neat black stitches holding it together.

"I removed four pounds of rocks from his stomach," Dr. Bucalo told Dana. "The rocks took up so much space that there was no room for actual food."

"Why do seals do that?" Dana wanted to know. "Why do they swallow rocks?"

"No one is certain. It's kind of a mystery," Dr. Bucalo replied. "Some scientists say seals think the rocks are ice, and eat them because they're thirsty. Others say seals swallow rocks for ballast, to help them dive deep. The seals may just be hungry, and if the rocks happen to be the right size to swallow . . ."

He shrugged. "All I can say is, eating rocks didn't do this little guy any good. He was well on his way to starving to death."

"Will he get better?" Dana asked.

"I hope so," said Dr. Bucalo. "We'll have to wait and see how he heals, and how long it takes him to start eating on his own."

Dana's mom stuck her head into the infirmary: "Hi. Where's Tyler?" she asked.

"He said he was going down to the bay to look at the kayaks," Dana told her. "Thanks, Dr. Bucalo," she added to the vet.

As they walked out of the office, Mrs. Chapin asked, "Is everything all right, sweetie?"

"I guess so," Dana said. "Tyler can be a pain."

"Dana, you have to remember that everything's new for him: Parsons Point, Neptune, Rockport Middle School, living with our family instead of his dad . . .

21

It's a lot for Tyler to deal with. Give him some time. I'm sure he'll come around." Mrs. Chapin turned toward the barn. "When you've finished your homework, maybe you can help your dad and me out here," she added. "We're cleaning some of the tanks."

"Sure," said Dana.

But as Dana opened the door to the house, she grumbled to herself, "What about *Tyler* being a lot for *me* to deal with? I'm used to being the only kid in the house, too. Plus he embarrasses me in front of my friends, he hangs around with the Motes, he doesn't help out at Neptune . . . he thinks he's so special! Like why isn't Tyler doing *his* homework right now?"

Dana dumped her backpack in her room and gave Jake a few dog treats. Then she decided to climb the steps of the lighthouse. She wanted to see what Tyler was up to.

When Dana reached the platform at the top of the tower, she edged around to stare down at the kayak rack on the bay beach. She sucked in her breath: Her kayak was missing!

Had Tyler paddled off by himself? Without a life vest?

Then Dana noticed a streak of bright purple out of the corner of her eye. She stood on tiptoe to peer past the rocky bank.

The purple kayak was resting on the sand a few feet from the water. Tyler was sitting in it with a paddle in his hand—and he was pretending he was paddling! He looked so silly that Dana started to giggle.

Then somebody in a green-and-white jacket leaned over to say something to Tyler. Was it one of the Motes?

No, this guy was much too tall.

The other person straightened up. Luke was with Tyler!

Dana hadn't liked it when Tyler didn't try to get along with her friends. But maybe she liked it even less when he *did* get along with them.

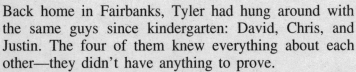

CHAPTER FOUR

Back home in Fairbanks, Tyler had hung around with the same guys since kindergarten: David, Chris, and Justin. The four of them knew everything about each other—they didn't have anything to prove.

But at Rockport Middle School, Tyler was faced with hundreds of kids he didn't know at all. They didn't know what kind of person he was, either.

Tyler really wasn't sure how to handle it.

Should he act as though he couldn't care less if anyone liked him or not? Which might make him *seem* cool. Or should he try hard to let the Rockport kids know exactly how cool he could be?

Tyler did it both ways on Monday at lunch with Dana's friends.

Neither way seemed to work. When Tyler didn't talk, they ignored him. And when he told them about the stuff he'd done back in Alaska, they thought he was showing off.

His classes were going to be okay: math, English, history, social studies, science—pretty much what he'd been taking back in Fairbanks.

But his Rockport social life might be a problem.

On Tuesday Tyler ate lunch by himself and wondered what Chris, Justin, and David were up to without him. He was definitely feeling down in the dumps.

Later that afternoon, though, Tyler met the Motes.

Tyler noticed Carter Mote first. At least, he noticed what Carter was doing, which wasn't the math problems Mr. Jackson had scrawled on the board.

Carter sat in the row next to Tyler's. He was wearing a shirt that looked like the top to somebody's old pajamas. And he was drawing amazing cartoons of superheroes and monsters and spaceships.

"Very cool!" Tyler whispered.

Carter just smiled. He didn't seem to be much of a talker. Carter didn't answer any questions in class, not even when Mr. Jackson called on him directly.

Math was the last class of the day for Tyler. When it was over he walked out of the room behind Carter Mote.

The hall was full of noisy kids milling around, getting ready to go home.

"Charlie," Carter said to Tyler.

"No, I'm Tyler," Tyler said.

"He means *I'm* Charlie," said another voice.

And there was a second boy, looking a lot like Carter. That wasn't surprising, since Charlie and Carter turned out to be twins.

Charlie was wearing a faded Army jacket about three sizes too big. And he did enough talking for him *and* his brother.

"We're twins, but we're not identical," Charlie said as he and Carter walked toward the side door of the building with Tyler. "Some kids think Carter's dumb, but he's not. He just doesn't have much to say to most people. It doesn't matter if he doesn't talk, anyway, because he's going to draw for a living. I'm going to be a fisherman, like my dad. Or a carpenter, if there aren't any fish left.''

''What do you mean, 'if there aren't any fish left'?'' Tyler asked.

''My dad says the seals eat them. Maybe they do eat some. But Carter and me think too many fish get caught by other people,'' Charlie said. ''There are gigundo ships not that far out in the ocean, Japanese and Russian ones—we've seen 'em—with drift nets forty miles long. Nothing can get past them.''

''Forty miles long? Wow!'' said Tyler, trying to imagine it.

He noticed that Charlie's feet had outgrown his shoes. A toe covered with a greenish sock stuck out the side of his left sneaker.

Charlie was already off and running on another subject.

''Did you see those guys snowboarding last night on MTV?'' he said. ''Sailed right off the edge of a monster mountain!''

Tyler nodded. He hadn't actually seen snowboarders the night before because nobody watched much TV at Parsons Point. But he *had* seen them on MTV and the sports channel at his real house. And his dad said he could try snowboarding himself when he was a year or two older.

''There's not enough snow around here for snowboarding. Or any mountains either, which is a major problem,'' Charlie added, grinning. ''But I'd like to try some of that extreme sports stuff. Like white-water kayaking. Or rock climbing without ropes. Or—''

"I've done some mountain climbing," Tyler said. "With ropes, though," he added quickly. He didn't want the Motes to think he was bragging.

"Where?" said Carter.

When Carter did talk, he stuck to one or two words.

"Alaska," Tyler said. "I'm from Alaska."

"Alaska!" said Charlie. "Cool! Have you seen grizzlies?"

Tyler nodded. "Lots of them. And wolves, too," he said. "My dad's living in the Arctic right now, studying wolves."

"Wow . . . ," said Carter.

"Living in an igloo?" Charlie asked.

"Who?" said Tyler, losing track of the conversation.

"Your dad, in the Arctic!" said Charlie.

"My dad in an igloo?" Tyler said. He tried to picture his six-foot-four father folded into a little round house made of ice cubes, and couldn't.

Tyler started to laugh.

Charlie and Carter laughed, too

"Extreme living," Charlie said.

"Very," said Tyler, still laughing.

It was the first time Tyler had laughed since he left Fairbanks. It felt good.

That's when Dana poked him in the back.

Then she practically dragged him onto their bus, sat him down, and told him a bunch of stuff about Charlie and Carter's dad fighting with Uncle Joe and Aunt Lissa over Project Neptune.

Tyler didn't see that it had anything to do with him, or with the Mote twins.

In fact, Tyler thought Dana might be using the fight as a handy excuse to make him stay away from the

Motes. He'd seen the way some of the kids looked at Charlie and Carter.

Maybe the twins dressed, or even acted, kind of different. But Tyler liked them better than anyone else he'd met so far in Rockport.

Then he had a disturbing thought. If what Dana said about her folks and Mr. Mote happened to be true . . . would the Mote twins feel differently about *him*?

Tyler hadn't mentioned his last name to Charlie and Carter. Once they found out he was a Chapin, they might not want to have anything more to do with him.

Tyler stood up and walked to the end of the bus to wave at the twins.

They waved back. Charlie growled and clawed at the air with his hands, like a grizzly bear.

Then the bus moved forward. Tyler sat down on the backseat.

He couldn't do extreme snowboarding or mountain climbing at Parsons Point. But there had to be other ways he could show Charlie and Carter and the Rockport kids that he wasn't some big-city geek.

The school bus turned onto Harbor Lane, and Tyler caught sight of Badger Bay. A north wind was whipping the water in the bay into small whitecaps. If Tyler squinted, he could almost imagine he was looking at white-water rapids on a really wide river.

Farther out, Tyler could see the string of dark gray rocks that formed Crab Island. And a thought started to form in his head . . . okay, kayaking to the island wouldn't exactly be extreme sports. The island wasn't that far away, and he wouldn't be shooting any rapids. But it was probably as extreme as Tyler could get around Rockport.

The school bus creaked to a stop. The doors swung open, and Dana stepped down.

Tyler jumped off the bus behind her. Dana was surprised when he turned toward the bay instead of the lighthouse.

"I won't try to paddle a kayak anywhere," Tyler said before Dana could open her mouth. He added under his breath, ". . . for now, anyway." Then he walked toward the rocky bank above the beach.

The wind blew straight into his face. The cold air smelled a little fishy, but fresh.

Tyler scrambled down the rocks to the kayak rack. The rack was made of iron pipes and bolted to the wooden pilings of Neptune's dock. The two kayaks were strapped to the rack upside down, to keep rain and sea spray out of them. Tyler tapped on their decking: Both were made of tough, molded plastic.

Tyler was unstrapping the purple kayak when he heard someone sliding down the rocks behind him.

"Dana, will you give me a break?" Tyler muttered crossly.

But it wasn't Dana. It was the high school guy Tyler had seen at Neptune the day he'd arrived.

"Hi, I'm Luke Bucalo," Luke said. "You're Tyler."

"Right," Tyler said. "The yellow kayak's yours?"

Luke nodded. "It's a little rough on the bay for kayaking, though," he said. "I was just making sure the wind hadn't blown the boats loose."

Then Luke noticed that Tyler had unfastened the straps on the purple kayak.

"But if you want to paddle along the shoreline, I'll go with you. The spray skirts are folded up in the bows

29

of the kayaks," Luke told Tyler. "The life vests are in the barn."

Luke is cool, Tyler decided. *He sure won't try to boss me around.*

"I don't know much about this yet," Tyler said to him. "Maybe you could give me some kayaking tips—on dry land."

"Sure," said Luke. "The basics are easy."

There was a two-part paddle strapped to Luke's kayak.

In a few minutes Luke had Tyler sitting in the cockpit of the purple kayak on the beach.

One end of a nylon spray skirt was snapped to the outside of the cockpit. The other end was tied snugly around Tyler's waist. The paddle was in Tyler's hands.

"These are touring kayaks, which means they're broader and flatter than white-water boats," Luke explained to Tyler. "They're a little harder to turn. But they're also faster and much less likely to tip over in heavy surf. And you won't be speeding through rapids at fifty miles an hour—not around here, anyway."

"Right," Tyler agreed.

He figured he'd mostly be going in a straight line: straight from this bay beach to Crab Island. Now that he was sitting in a kayak at water level, the island looked quite a bit farther away than it had from the lighthouse.

Luke showed Tyler how to hold the paddle. "Since you're right-handed, that'll be your control hand," he said. "Your control hand never moves on the paddle. Your left hand will be your slip hand. It'll loosen between strokes, and move up and down the shaft of the paddle as you need it to."

"Got it," Tyler said. He slid his left hand up and down as he raised or lowered the paddle with his right.

Then Luke showed Tyler different kayaking strokes: the power stroke, the forward sweep, the rudder, and the draw.

"We'll save the body moves until we get you into the water," Luke told Tyler. "Like the brace. And the Eskimo roll—that'll right your kayak if you've flipped over. But you said you've canoed, so you'll pick up kayaking in no time."

"Tyler!" Suddenly Dana was standing on the rocks above them.

Luke waved at Dana. Tyler didn't move.

"Tyler!" Dana yelled over the wind. "Mom wants us to do our homework right now, so we can help out with the seals."

"We're gonna run out of light soon, anyway," Luke said to Tyler, pointing toward the sinking sun.

Tyler sighed. He loosened the spray skirt so he could climb out of the kayak.

"I've got an excellent book about kayaking. The drawings make everything really clear," Luke said to him. "I'll send the book over to Neptune tomorrow with my dad."

"Great!" Tyler said.

He picked up one end of the purple kayak, and Luke picked up the other. They carried it to the rack and slid it into place.

Tyler was going to help Luke strap the kayak down when Dana called "TYYYLER!" again.

"I'll strap it," Luke said to him.

"I'm coming!" Tyler shouted to his cousin. "Thanks a lot, Luke," he added.

"No problem—see you around," said Luke.

CHAPTER FIVE

Dana practically flew down the stairs at the lighthouse, threw on her jacket, and raced down the gravel road.

There Tyler was, with Luke, hanging out beside the bay, while she was supposed to be sitting in the house doing her homework, and then cleaning exercise tanks in the barn—definitely not her favorite chore.

"No way," Dana mumbled to herself from the rocks above the bay beach. "Tyler's going to help out, too."

Okay, so her parents hadn't exactly said anything about Tyler's homework, or about him working in the barn. But they should have said it.

When Dana yelled for him, Tyler grabbed his backpack and climbed the rocks pretty fast.

"What's wrong with you?" Tyler asked when he reached her.

"Nothing's wrong!" Dana said. She whirled around and marched back toward the house.

"Well, you sure act like something's wrong," Tyler said, catching up with her. "You're mad because I sat in your kayak," he guessed.

Which sounded totally dumb.

"I'm not mad," Dana said, trying hard not to sound mad.

"Okay," Tyler said. He seemed to be in a good mood. He even started humming to himself. But he didn't say anything else on the way to the house, and neither did Dana.

When she shoved the back door open, Jake came bounding over to say hello—to Tyler.

"Hey, boy—I missed you, too," Tyler said, giving the dog a hug. "Hi, Aunt Lissa," he added as Dana's mom strolled into the kitchen.

"Well, where have you two been?" she asked, sounding pleased at the thought of the cousins doing something together.

"Oh, we were just looking at the bay and the kayaks," Tyler said smoothly. "We came in to do our homework. And then we'll help you out in the barn."

"That would be terrific, Tyler!" Mrs. Chapin exclaimed.

She looked at Dana and smiled, as if to say, See? I told you Tyler would come around if you gave him a chance.

Tyler glanced at Dana, too.

Dana knew *his* look meant, Gotcha! It wasn't your mom and dad's idea for me to come into the house. It was yours!

But Tyler didn't say anything to give her away.

Dana and Tyler got started on their reports for social studies. Dana showed him the on-line encyclopedia on the computer in the living room. Later Tyler helped her with a math problem—he was good at math.

33

Then they walked over to the barn, where Tyler really worked hard that afternoon.

Dana and Tyler, and Sue Larkin and Tim Gilmore, a couple of Neptuners, drained all three of the exercise tanks with submersible pumps and hoses.

"Now we need buckets and squeegees," Dana told Tyler, opening the steel supply cabinet near the sliding door.

"What are the wet suits for?" Tyler asked her, peering into the cabinet.

"Sometimes we have to climb into the tanks to help a weak animal swim," Dana said. "The water's practically freezing at this time of year. We couldn't do it without wet suits."

She and Tyler scrubbed out a couple of the exercise tanks with bleach, which always made Dana's eyes water and her nose run.

Dana explained how important it was to keep everything that the animals might touch really clean. "Lots of times stranded animals are too weak to fight off germs," she said to Tyler. "Bleach kills bacteria and viruses."

Then they refilled the tanks, and Dana let Ellie dive into one for a swim. This time Tyler paid some attention to the little blind seal as she glided happily around.

"She's not really gray," he murmured to Dana. "She's silver."

" 'Grey' is the kind of seal she is," Dana said. "Like 'harbor,' and 'hooded.' "

"How many of these guys are there in the world?" Tyler wanted to know.

"Not many," Tim Gilmore told him. "They were hunted so much in the last century that they were

34

thought to be extinct in North America. Then a small group turned up in New Brunswick.''

"They're fully protected in the United States now, but they're still killing them in Canada," Sue Larkin added.

The thought made Dana queasy. How could anybody kill Ellie?

"Grey seals travel thousands of miles each year," Tim went on. "They can dive as deep as seven hundred feet."

"Wow! How big do they get?" Tyler asked, watching Ellie do a jackknife.

"The males grow to more than seven feet," Sue said. "They can weigh almost five hundred pounds, the females a little less."

"So wherever she ends up, Ellie's going to need a full-size swimming pool," Tyler said.

Dana thought Tyler might actually be starting to get interested in what happened around Neptune. Maybe having him at Parsons Point wouldn't be so bad after all.

But if Dana believed an interest in Neptune would keep Tyler away from the Mote twins, she was wrong. At lunch the very next day, Tyler sat with Charlie and Carter in the cafeteria.

"Look who your cousin's hanging out with," Jason said to Dana as she set her tray down at their regular table.

Cassie stared at Tyler and the Motes and wrinkled her nose. "Yuck," she said. "I don't think I could eat anything, sitting that close to Carter Mote."

Even Kim shook her head.

But what could Dana do about it?

One thing I can do is talk to Mom and Dad, Dana told herself.

And she did talk to them that evening, once Tyler had gone to his room to listen to CDs on his disc player.

"Tyler's hanging around with Charlie and Carter Mote," Dana said to her folks in the kitchen. "I explained about us and Mr. Mote. But Tyler doesn't think it has anything to do with him."

"Tyler's right, Dana," her dad said. "It doesn't have anything to do with the twins, either. It's not even us against Wilbur Mote. Lots of people don't want to face the facts about overfishing."

"Or water pollution, or everything else that's bad for this environment," said her mother.

"It's so much easier to blame seals," Mr. Chapin said. "But Project Neptune will hang in there, and maybe someday we'll change even Mr. Mote's way of thinking."

"You have to let Tyler choose his own friends, Dana," her mom added. "Who knows? Some of Neptune's ideas may rub off on Charlie and Carter through Tyler."

I hope Charlie and Carter don't rub off on Tyler instead, Dana said to herself.

CHAPTER SIX

Tyler told the Mote twins he was a Chapin the first chance he got, when they ate lunch together the next day.

Carter shrugged. He was busy sketching a space alien on his napkin.

Charlie said, "So . . . we just can't visit you at the lighthouse."

And that was the end of that.

The twins knew a lot about Crab Island.

"We've sailed past it a hundred times in our dad's boat," Charlie said.

"Shallow," said Carter.

"Yeah, there are sandbars all around it, stretching out a quarter of a mile or so. Big boats can't get too close to Crab Island, or they'll run aground," Charlie explained. "Most places, the water's too shallow for outboards, even. And the depth changes all the time. Waves and tides move the bottom around."

The shallow water wouldn't matter to Tyler, since he'd be in a kayak.

"Shipwrecks," Carter added.

"Yeah, Dad told us that lots of ships wrecked on those rocks in the old days," said Charlie. "There could even be some treasure there! But with the waves and currents—"

Tyler was getting really excited. He might find swords or muskets, maybe silver and gold coins on Crab Island! And even if he didn't find anything, it would still be an incredible adventure.

"I'm going!" he said to the twins in a low voice.

"See you," said Carter. He thought Tyler meant he was leaving the cafeteria.

"No, no—I'm going to Crab Island!" Tyler told them.

Carter stopped drawing to stare at him.

"How are you gonna do that?" said Charlie. "It's too far for you to row a boat—too heavy."

"But not for a plastic kayak," Tyler said.

"A kayak might just work," Charlie said thoughtfully.

"Currents," Carter pointed out.

"The kayak is so light it'll float right over them," Tyler said. At least he was hoping it would.

"Waves break across Crab Island sometimes," Charlie warned him.

"I heard. I'll wait until there's a nice, calm day," said Tyler.

"This would be so cool—the coolest thing anyone's ever done in the history of Rockport Middle School!" said Charlie.

If Tyler had had any doubts at all about paddling to the island, Charlie Mote had just settled them.

After school that afternoon, Tyler took the bus home, but Dana went to her friend Kim's house.

Tyler stopped by the clinic to pick up Luke's kay-aking book from Dr. Bucalo.

The little hooded seal from Indian Beach was lying flat on his side, but he was awake. He gazed out of his cage with moist, perfectly round eyes, and sighed deeply when he saw Tyler.

"He won't be able to eat solid food for a while," Dr. Bucalo told Tyler. "But his temperature's down. I think he's going to make it."

The veterinarian tapped a photograph on the wall next to the cage. "Here's what this little fellow will look like in four or five years," Dr. Bucalo said. "You can see why they're called 'hooded'."

"Yow!" said Tyler.

In the photo two huge hooded seals were facing one another on an ice floe. Both of them had what looked like big brown footballs squashed down on the tops of their heads. If that wasn't strange enough, a bright red balloony thing hung out of one nostril of each of their noses.

"What's that red balloon for?" Tyler said to Dr. Bucalo.

"They're just making themselves as handsome as possible for the females," Dr. Bucalo said with a smile.

Tyler glanced at the little seal in the cage again. "Poor guy," he murmured. "You really have a lot to look forward to." He had to admit, seals were more interesting than he'd imagined.

"Does he have a name yet?" Tyler asked Dr. Bucalo.

"Mr. Garber wants to call him Elvis," the veterinarian said with a laugh. "He thinks the hoods look a little like Elvis Presley's pompadour."

"Elvis," said Tyler. "Cool."

Dr. Bucalo handed Tyler *Kayaking Basics*. Then Tyler walked over to the barn. There were four or five Neptuners there, cleaning cages and mopping the concrete floor. Uncle Joe and Aunt Lissa were talking to two women at the far end of the barn. They didn't notice Tyler when he opened the doors to the steel supply cabinet.

"What are you looking for?" an older girl in a padded jacket asked him.

"Life vests?" Tyler said.

"They're in the metal trunk behind the tanks," she told him.

"Thanks," Tyler said, heading for the sliding door instead.

"Hey, do you want a vest or not?" the girl called out.

Tyler shook his head. "Just checking," he said.

Now Tyler knew where to find just about everything he needed. The wet suits were in the cabinet with the mops and buckets. It would be way too cold to paddle to Crab Island without a wet suit on under his clothes. Life vests were in a metal trunk. The spray skirt was in the kayak.

He would like to find another paddle, though. Luke said it was always a good idea to take two paddles on a kayaking trip, in case one of them got away from you. And Tyler sure didn't want to be suddenly paddleless on a trip to Crab Island.

He wondered where Dana kept hers.

Tyler hurried back to the house. Jake followed him around while he looked in the closet in Dana's room, under her bed, and in the kitchen.

Two paddles—Dana's and an extra—turned up in the hall closet.

Now Tyler had it covered: kayak, wet suit, life vest, spray skirt, and a couple of paddles. All he had to do was study Luke's book.

And he needed a calm, sunny day, of course.

Tyler headed for his room, ready to dive into *Kayaking Basics*. Then he noticed his dad's picture on the chest of drawers, and he felt a little guilty.

Tyler hadn't written to his father since he'd arrived at Parsons Point.

Not that his dad could get mail more than once a month, when a small seaplane delivered supplies to the weather station where he was staying. But Tyler had promised that he'd write a letter weekly and tell his father about everything he'd seen and done. His dad said he'd do the same.

Tyler went back into the living room and sat down at the computer.

He began the letter,

Hi Dad,

I got here okay—it took twenty-three hours. Uncle Joe met me at the airport, and then we drove straight to Parsons Point. It's not very scenic here—it's really flat. But the lighthouse is kind of cool, almost two hundred years old.

Uncle Joe and Aunt Lissa look just the way I remembered them from California. Dana has changed a lot, though. She's not as skinny as she was. Her hair is long, and she is always messing with it. She's kind of bossy, and sometimes she minds my business. I don't think she likes having me here that much.

*School is okay. Classes at Rockport Middle
School aren't that different from classes at White
Mountains Middle School. I've made two friends,
Charlie and Carter Mote. They're twins, even though
they don't look exactly alike. One of them talks, and
the other mostly draws. Charlie, the one who talks,
wanted to know if you lived in an igloo! Where do
you live? Is it a house, or a trailer, or what?*

*How are you doing anyway? How many wolves
are in the pack you're studying? Are you videotaping
them? The seals here at Project Neptune are pretty
interesting. One of them ate a lot of rocks and almost
starved to death—he is a hooded seal. When they're
adults, male hooded seals grow giant brown pillows
on their heads, and blow gross red balloons out of
their noses to make the female seals like them.*

Tyler started to write something about Luke and kayaking, but he back-spaced it out. He didn't want to give
anything away about his trip to Crab Island, not yet,
not even to his father.

Instead he wrote,

*I'm planning kind of a cool surprise—more like
an adventure . . .*

Tyler paused again.

He knew his dad wouldn't see this letter for three or
four weeks at least. Still . . .

*I won't say what it is yet, but it's going to be
totally awesome. And I'll be doing it soon. I'll let
you know as soon as I've pulled it off.*

That's all for now. I'll write again next week. Stay warm, Dad.

                                    Love, Tyler.

He was about to print out his letter when his uncle's voice called from the back door: "Tyler, are you in here?"

"At the computer, Uncle Jim," Tyler answered.

"Can you give me a hand in the barn?" his uncle said.

"Sure," said Tyler.

He saved his letter under "WOLF," pushed his chair back, and grabbed his jacket from the coat rack.

"Coming!" Tyler said.

CHAPTER SEVEN

Dana was almost certain her cousin was up to something.

For one thing, he was suddenly in a better mood, not moping around like he had been. For another, he was acting a little too thoughtful as far as Dana was concerned.

That afternoon after school, Dana had told Tyler she wouldn't be taking the bus home because she was going over to Kim's house.

Kim said, "Dana'll be staying for dinner." Then she added politely, "Tyler, you can come, too, if you want."

"Oh, no thanks," Tyler said quickly. "I know I've been taking up a lot of Dana's time. It's great that she'll have a chance to spend a few hours with a friend."

And Tyler trotted off toward the bus.

"That sounded kind of lame, didn't it?" Dana said, staring after her cousin. "Like he couldn't wait to get rid of me. Do you think he's doing something he doesn't want me to know about?"

"What could Tyler do in Rockport that you couldn't know about?" said Kim sensibly. "Maybe he's just being nice about you needing time for your own life."

Dana shook her head and thought for a second.

"The Motes!" she exclaimed. "I'll bet Tyler's sneaking off to get into trouble with the Mote twins!"

"Uh-uh, try again. I saw Charlie and Carter drive away with their father a few minutes ago," Kim said. "Hey, there's Dad in the van. Come on."

Mr. Meyers rolled down the window of his red van and called out, "Hi, Dana. Long time no see. Girls, watch out for the cameras," he warned as Kim reached for the side door. "They're on the floor back there, along with a tripod."

Kim's mom and dad never went anywhere without a couple of video cameras, just in case they came across a news story in the making. They managed WLIR, the small Rockport television station.

"Dana, I was hoping to meet that cousin of yours. His name is Tyler, isn't it?" Mr. Meyers went on as he drove out of the parking lot. "Maybe we could do a short interview with him: find out how a visitor from Alaska likes our town."

"Oh, Dad, how embarrassing," Kim murmured.

"It definitely would be," Dana said to her friend in a low voice. "We already *know* what Tyler thinks about Rockport—nothing good. I'm sure he'd leave here tomorrow if he could."

But it wasn't until she and Kim were sitting in Kim's bedroom, munching on trail mix and watching TV, that Dana put two and two together.

Kim was holding the remote. She clicked on a movie

45

about teenage runaways: Two kids were climbing on a bus to Los Angeles in the middle of the night.

"That's it!" Dana said suddenly, pointing at the screen

"What?" said Kim.

"Something tells me that Tyler's made up his mind to run away!" Dana said.

"To Los Angeles?" said Kim, puzzled, staring at the TV.

"No, back home to Alaska!" Dana said.

"Why would you think that?" Kim asked her.

"He's been acting weird. Like pretending he's interested in Neptune, when just a few days ago he thought saving seals was a total waste of time," said Dana. "And he's helping out around the barn, too, without complaining. I'll bet it's all an act to throw us off the track!"

"I don't see how one thing leads to another," said Kim. "Anyway, how would Tyler get back to Alaska? Hitchhike?" She giggled because she wasn't taking Dana seriously. "He'd be traveling for months!"

"Tyler has money—money that Uncle Jim gave him to buy stuff while he's living with us," Dana said firmly. "Mom and Dad are going to open a bank account for him, but they haven't had time yet. So Tyler could use that money to take a bus to the airport in Wilton and pay for a plane ticket to Fairbanks."

"I don't know, Dana," said Kim doubtfully.

Dana had to admit that she didn't have any real, solid proof—at least, not until she got home that evening.

Kim and Mrs. Meyers dropped Dana off at Parsons Point around nine o'clock.

Tyler was already in his room with the door closed.

"He's reading a book Luke lent him," Mrs. Chapin told her daughter.

He's probably packing, Dana said to herself.

"I'm glad Tyler and Luke are becoming friends," Dana's dad added.

Dana had too much on her mind to get upset again about Tyler hanging around with Luke.

"Did you finish your homework at Kim's?" her mother asked.

"Just about. I want to print out what I've written so far for social studies," Dana said.

She walked into the living room and sat down at the computer.

But when Dana pulled the word processing files onto the computer screen, her eye was caught by a new file: "WOLF."

"What could that be?" she murmured.

It only took her a second to find out.

"WOLF" was a letter from Tyler to his dad.

Dana knew it was wrong for her to read the letter. But she just couldn't help herself. Maybe it would give her a clue to what Tyler was planning.

" 'Dear Dad: I got here okay . . . ,' " Dana read.

She skimmed the first paragraph and didn't learn anything new. As she'd said to Kim, she already had a pretty good idea about what Tyler thought of Parsons Point.

She went on to the second paragraph.

"I'm not as skinny as I was?" Dana stopped reading to protest. "What's that supposed to mean? That I'm fat now? And I'm *not* always messing with my hair!"

As soon as she said it, she smoothed her hair back behind her ears.

47

Dana read on. "*I'm* bossy? Look who's talking!" she muttered. "And I don't mind his business. Who would want to mind Tyler Chapin's business? Too borrrring!"

Then Dana read the next sentence: " 'I don't think she likes having me here that much. . . .' "

Which stopped Dana short for a moment.

Tyler was right. And if he'd noticed that, maybe he wasn't quite so wrapped up in himself as she'd thought.

Dana went on reading, about the Mote twins and about hooded seals.

Then she sucked in her breath. She'd gotten to the part of the letter where Tyler mentioned a cool surprise that he was planning: "more like an adventure," he'd written.

" 'I won't say what it is yet, but it's going to be totally awesome. I'll be doing it soon. . . ,' " Tyler had written.

A surprise . . . an adventure . . . totally awesome . . .

"This is it!" Dana murmured. "Tyler's planning to run away—go back to Alaska! And soon!"

She stood up, ready to rush into the kitchen to tell her parents everything.

But then Dana sat back down.

What could she really tell them?

For starters, Dana would have to admit to her mom and dad that she'd been reading Tyler's private mail—not a good idea.

Plus, in his letter, Tyler never actually *said* he was running away from Parsons Point. So he might be able to twist the words around to mean something else altogether. And Dana would end up sounding nosy and ridiculous.

What could she do?

One thing popped into her mind right away.

Dana walked quietly into the hall. She picked up the phone and dialed the Harbor Bus Company in Rockport.

"Can you please tell me what times your buses leave for Wilton?" Dana asked the lady who answered.

"Certainly," the lady said. "There's only one bus a day to Wilton, and it leaves here at 10:40 every morning."

"Thank you," Dana said.

Keeping tabs on Tyler every morning until 10:40 shouldn't be that hard, should it?

On weekdays, he'd be in school.

And on weekends . . . Dana would be around to catch him in the act!

CHAPTER EIGHT

All that week Tyler studied Luke's kayaking book. He practiced different strokes in his room, using a broom for a paddle.

Tyler thought he'd do a few trial runs along the bay shore as soon as he could. He'd have to keep one eye on the weather. And the other eye on Dana.

When Tyler woke up on Saturday, the day was sunny, calm, and warm.

"January thaw," Uncle Joe said over breakfast. "It feels like spring. You kids should take advantage of the good weather while it lasts. You could go hiking, or rock climbing. . . ."

Or kayaking, Tyler said to himself. He was afraid there would be way too many people around, though.

"Aren't you and Mom driving over to Bellvale to Hardware Depot?" Dana said to her father. "I'd like to go with you."

Yesss! Tyler said to himself.

"But—" Uncle Joe began.

"I need some school stuff, and Bellvale Stationery

has very cool notebooks—they've got holograms on the covers,'' Dana said.

"Well—'' Uncle Joe glanced at Tyler.

"I'll be fine, Uncle Joe,'' Tyler said. "There'll be plenty of Neptuners around. I'll hang out with Luke, or help in the barn, or something.''

Dana was watching him out of the corner of her eye.

Tyler smiled at her. He just couldn't believe his luck. He knew Luke had an out-of-town basketball game, and that Luke's folks were going to watch him play. And while there might be some Neptuners at Parsons Point, Dana would be busy in Bellvale, buying notebooks.

He'd have a few hours entirely to himself to practice in the kayak.

As soon as Dana drove away from the Point with Uncle Joe and Aunt Lissa, Tyler hurried to the barn. He stopped for a moment to say hello to Ellie. But the little grey seal had a full stomach, and she was sound asleep, snoring peacefully.

He waved to Tim Gilmore, who was feeding Harold and Maude. When Tim wasn't looking, Tyler eased a life vest out of the trunk behind the exercise tanks. He snagged one of the smaller wet suits from the steel supply cabinet. Then he raced back to the lighthouse.

Jake padded down the hall behind Tyler to the bedroom.

Tyler stripped off his clothes and pulled on the wet suit.

Even with all of the zippers zipped, the wet suit was a little loose in spots. But Tyler figured that was okay. He didn't intend to go swimming in it—he just wanted it to keep him warm while he did a practice run in the kayak.

Tyler put his clothes on again over the wet suit. He chose a wool shirt instead of his sweatshirt, and put sneakers on over the wet suit booties. Then Tyler squeezed into his jacket.

He felt like an overstuffed pillow. But he'd probably be warm enough for the Arctic.

"If anything," Tyler said to himself, "I'll roast in this outfit."

He took the extra paddle out of the hall closet and picked up the life vest. He opened the back door of the house a crack and stuck his head out. When he was sure there was no one in sight, Tyler edged around behind the lighthouse.

Keeping the lighthouse between himself and the other buildings at Parsons Point, he headed for the rocky bank above the bay beach.

Tyler had scrambled down the rocks when he realized he wasn't alone: Jake the dog was only a few yards behind him.

"Jake, go home!" Tyler ordered loudly, waving his arms.

Jake grinned and trotted around him, down to the bay. The dog waded into saltwater up to his belly, his tail wagging.

"How cold is it, Boy?" Tyler said. As bundled up as he was, it almost felt like summer to him.

But when he stuck his hand into Badger Bay, his fingers went numb. He jerked his hand right back out again.

"Majorly cold!" Tyler said, then added, "No big deal—I just won't fall out of the boat." He walked over to the kayak rack and started unstrapping the purple kayak.

Jake trotted out of the water, too, shaking himself dry. He wandered down the beach to flush a crab out of a big clump of seaweed.

Tyler pulled Dana's kayak off the rack, turned it upright on the sand, and reached into the bow for the spray skirt.

He snapped the skirt onto the outside of the kayak's cockpit. Then he unhooked the two-part paddle from Luke's kayak. He fastened the paddle to the back of his own boat with the deck lines.

Tyler slipped into the life vest and zipped it up.

"Well," he said, taking a deep breath of salty air, "I guess I'm ready to ride!"

He dragged the purple kayak across the narrow beach to the water. He slowly shoved it forward.

The kayak bobbed like a cork just a foot or so from shore.

"Cool," Tyler murmured.

He picked up the paddle from the hall closet. Then he stepped into the kayak from shore, just like in *Kayaking Basics*: ". . . one foot into the cockpit, sit down on the back deck, other foot into the cockpit, and quickly slide your body in."

Under Tyler's weight, the light little boat sank several inches, until it rested on the sandy bottom of the bay. Tyler shoved against the sand with the edge of his paddle. And he was floating!

He tied the spray skirt tight around his waist. Then he stroked the water with his paddle a few times—right, left, right, left. The purple boat went scooting across the surface of the bay.

"Excellent," said Tyler. "I just might be a natural kayaker."

He steered close to shore, heading toward the tip of Parsons Point. Tyler had planned to make at least a couple of trips up and down the shoreline that morning, trying out different strokes. Maybe he'd even tip his kayak over to see if he could flip it upright again.

But as he glided closer to the tip of Parsons Point, Tyler was moving closer to Crab Island as well.

The island didn't seem nearly as far away as it had when he'd sat in the kayak on the beach with Luke. There were hardly any waves around the island, either— just little wavelets lapping at the bottoms of the gray boulders.

The sun was shining. The air was warm. Badger Bay looked as calm and smooth as a small pond. And there were no fishing boats to run into him. There wasn't a boat in sight in any direction; did fishermen take Saturdays off?

And a thought popped into Tyler's mind: *Why not go for it?*

Dana and her parents would be gone all afternoon. Luke and his mom and dad were out of town at a basketball game.

And how long could it take Tyler to paddle to Crab Island, explore the place, maybe pick up some souvenir trinkets, and paddle back?

Not more than a couple of hours, tops.

"I'm gonna do it!" Tyler said out loud.

His heart was pounding.

"Charlie and Carter will be blown away by this, and so will everybody else!" Tyler added.

A few strokes with his paddle on the left side of the boat, and the bow of Tyler's kayak was pointed straight at Crab Island.

Tyler started paddling strongly and evenly—right side, left side, right side, left. It was easy, so easy that Tyler couldn't believe nobody had made the trip before.

The purple boat slipped farther and farther away from shore, into Badger Bay.

Before long, Tyler began to get hot. He was paddling hard, and the sun was almost directly above him, beating down on his head and his shoulders. He was thinking about how hard it would be to take his jacket off in the kayak when a light breeze sprang up. It blew into Tyler's face and cooled him off.

The breeze grew a little stronger, rippling the waters of Badger Bay. It got harder for Tyler to travel in a straight line toward the island, as the wind tried to blow him off course.

Tyler remembered a drawing in Luke's kayak book. It showed how to angle a boat so that it wasn't facing straight into the wind. Tyler turned the bow of the kayak a fraction to the right, making it easier for him to paddle forward.

But he'd barely worked that out when suddenly the kayak seemed to be moving on its own. It felt as though a swift, invisible river were running just below the surface, and it had grabbed hold of the little boat. Something was carrying Tyler along, pushing him out toward the ocean. He'd met the current the Motes and Dana had warned him about. Tyler had to dig his paddle deep into the water to force the kayak toward Crab Island again.

The wind grew stronger. Little waves smacked against the kayak, splashing Tyler with icy water. Soon the sleeves of Tyler's jacket were wet and heavy.

Tyler squinted at Crab. Much larger waves were

crashing against those gray boulders, and he was starting to worry about his landing. The molded-plastic kayak probably wouldn't break against a rock. But Tyler might.

The sky was streaked with fast-moving clouds, and the wind was blowing hard. Larger waves washed over the bow of the kayak, soaking the rest of Tyler's jacket. For the first time that day, he was feeling the cold.

"The weather doesn't change this fast in Alaska," Tyler mumbled uneasily. Parsons Point wasn't nearly so tame as he'd thought.

And the current was still pushing fiercely against the kayak, threatening to shove it into the ocean.

The muscles in Tyler's arms were starting to burn.

"I must be halfway to the island by now," he said loudly, to cheer himself up.

Tyler swiveled around in his seat to look back at Parsons Point . . . and his heart almost stopped!

Not too far behind him, a yellow head bobbed up and down just inches above the dark blue swells.

Jake! He'd swum after Tyler, across Badger Bay.

Tyler knew he should paddle straight for Crab Island while he still had the strength. But he couldn't abandon Jake.

Every few seconds, a wave would surge over Jake's head, and the dog would disappear under water. Then he would struggle to the surface again. But Jake would soon be too tired to keep himself afloat.

Unless Tyler helped the dog, Jake would drown.

And Tyler would have himself to blame for it. He should have taken Jake back to the lighthouse and locked the dog inside before he'd climbed into the kayak.

Tyler stuck his paddle deep into the water. He made a broad, sweeping stroke on the left side of the purple boat. It turned the kayak almost completely around. One more stroke, and the bow of the boat was pointed at Jake.

"Hang on, Boy!" Tyler yelled.

It was hard going. Tyler had to fight across the current, through foaming waves that crashed over him and the kayak.

By the time Tyler reached the dog, Jake had barely enough strength to tread water.

When he saw Tyler, though, the panic in his eyes turned to relief.

"I'm going to help you, Jake!" Tyler yelled over the wind and the waves.

But how? There was no way Tyler could squeeze the dog into the narrow cockpit of the kayak with him. Jake was too heavy for Tyler to lift out of the water, anyway.

Maybe Tyler could tie a deck line from the kayak around Jake's body and pull him to land.

But Tyler didn't know if he was strong enough to paddle through the current dragging a seventy-pound dog along with him. And he wasn't at all certain that Jake could keep his nose above water much longer, either.

Jake had his own ideas. The dog was thrashing now, trying to hurl himself up out of the water. Before Tyler realized what Jake was doing, the dog had lunged upward and somehow clawed himself onto the bow of the kayak!

The little boat rocked dangerously. If the kayak flipped over, it would dump both Tyler and Jake into the churning, freezing waters of Badger Bay.

Tyler grabbed for Jake's collar, hoping he could calm the dog enough to make him lie quietly across the bow. That's when his paddle slipped out of Tyler's hand.

Jake's front legs were dangling off one side of the bow, his back legs off the other. He lay fairly still for a moment, shivering and trying to catch his breath.

Keeping one hand on the exhausted dog, Tyler reached behind the cockpit for Luke's two-part paddle.

Which way should he and Jake go?

Back toward Parsons Point?

Or on to Crab Island?

The current answered the question for Tyler: It was still pushing the kayak away from the Point.

Tyler jammed the two parts of the paddle together. Then he stuck one end of it straight down into the water to swing them around.

"Crab Island or bust!" Tyler shouted to cheer himself on.

Jake's tail wagged weakly.

But Tyler was scared.

CHAPTER NINE

Dana had her own plan that morning.

She didn't really intend to go to Bellvale to the stationery store.

She just wanted Tyler to *think* she was going.

She knew Luke had a basketball game, and with all three Chapins out of Tyler's way as well, this could be the day that her cousin tried to take a bus to the Wilton airport.

After breakfast Dana said good-bye to Jake and climbed into the truck with her folks.

They bumped across the Point to the main road. Dana waited until her father had driven a mile or so down Harbor Lane, to make certain they were out of sight of the lighthouse.

Then Dana said, "Dad, you know what? I think you're right. It's such nice weather, maybe I'd rather do something outdoors than go shopping in Bellvale."

"Good for you, sweetie," her dad said, slowing down and pulling over on the side of the road. "We'll take you right back to the house. . . ."

"Oh, no, that's okay, Dad," Dana said quickly. "I'll walk."

She certainly didn't want Tyler to see—or hear—the truck returning.

Mrs. Chapin opened the door of the truck and let Dana slide out. "You and Tyler have fun," she said. "We'll get back some time after lunch."

Dana waved to her parents. Once they'd disappeared around a curve, she glanced at her watch.

"It's around nine-fifteen," Dana said to herself. "Tyler will have to leave the Point right away if he wants to hike into Rockport in time to catch the 10:40 bus."

Dana jogged back up Harbor Lane, keeping a sharp eye out for her cousin. It didn't take her long to reach the gravel road that crossed Parsons Point. She crouched down behind the mailboxes and peered at the lighthouse.

So far there were no signs of Tyler making his get-away, hurrying toward the road with his backpack stuffed full.

Staying low, Dana dashed to the barn.

Noiselessly, she slipped through a side door.

Tim Gilmore and a couple of other Neptuners were busy doing chores. Ellie was swimming in her tank: Her hind flippers suddenly appeared above the rim as she jackknifed.

Then Tim spotted Dana.

"Dana, can you give me a hand with this spare cage?" he said in a loud whisper. "The door's jammed, and I'm trying to fix it."

"Oh. Sure," said Dana.

She helped Tim straighten out the cage door with pliers and replace some worn screws.

60

While they worked on the cage, Dana kept running to a window to stare over at the lighthouse or down the gravel road.

"What are you looking for?" Tim finally asked her.

"Um . . . I was just wondering where Tyler was," she said.

"Laurie," Tim murmured to another Neptuner, "didn't you say Tyler was in here earlier?"

"That's right. He grabbed a life vest and left," Laurie said in a low voice.

"A life vest?" Dana repeated. "To take a bus?" That didn't make sense.

And then she remembered Tyler and the kayaks. Wouldn't it be just like him to ignore every warning she'd given him?

He's probably paddling around somewhere by himself! Dana thought. "Gotta go!" she said to Tim as she hurried for the door.

First she checked inside her house: no Tyler.

And no Jake, either. The dog loved to tag along with the boats when Dana and Luke were kayaking! He'd trot beside them on the bank, chasing crabs and snapping at minnows.

And there was only one kayak paddle in the hall closet.

Dana ran down to the bay.

Tyler and Jake weren't on the beach. Neither was her purple kayak.

A web of narrow inlets led away from Badger Bay, winding through marshes and bogs. Tyler could have paddled up any one of them.

"I'll bet I can spot him from the tower!" Dana said. She sprinted back to the house. She grabbed her mom's binoculars off the coat rack in the hall and climbed the iron steps of the tower two at a time.

Dana arrived at the top of the lighthouse puffing and panting. She edged around the platform until she was facing away from the ocean, toward the head of the bay. It was going to take her awhile to pick out Tyler and Jake. There were dozens of inlets, even a small river, the Cupsogue, to check out.

Dana lifted the binoculars to her eyes and started scanning the bay shore.

But she didn't come across any splashes of color that would mean a purple kayak or an orange life vest. And Jake, who was the color of the dry winter grasses, would be even harder to see.

Wind had begun to rattle the old windows in the tower and kick the waters of Badger Bay into small whitecaps.

But the water in the inlets is a lot calmer, Dana told herself. "Tyler shouldn't have any trouble," she said out loud.

If Tyler did flip her kayak over somehow, the inlets were so shallow that he could wade to shore.

Dana turned, pointing the binoculars at Crab Island to see how big the waves were out there.

That's when she got the shock of her life!

A little more than halfway between Parsons Point and the gray rocks of the island, she spotted something narrow and purple, beneath something small, square, and orange, bobbing among the large, breaking waves.

With shaky hands, Dana refocused the binoculars, sharpening the images.

"Tyler!" she murmured breathlessly. "And Jake!"

She could see Tyler trying to keep Jake from slipping

62

off the bow, while he paddled toward Crab Island at the same time. Powerful waves tossed the little purple boat into the air, then flung it down, again and again.

"How can they ever make it to the island?" Dana groaned.

With every wave, she was certain the kayak would flip over, dumping the boy and the dog into the cold, choppy bay. And if the water didn't drown them right away, the cold would surely kill them.

Later Dana couldn't even remember running down the steps of the lighthouse. But the next thing she knew, she was grabbing the paddle out of the hall closet. Her blue life vest was tucked in there, too.

She yanked the blankets off her bed. She wrapped a box of kitchen matches inside a plastic bag so they wouldn't get wet, and stuck them in her pocket.

"No time to go to the barn for help," Dana mumbled to herself. She wasn't sure any of these Neptuners knew how to kayak, anyway.

But Dana did take a second to scrawl: "Mom and Dad—*CRAB ISLAND!!!*" on the little message board next to the stranding phone.

Then she threw on her jacket and the life vest.

With blankets under one arm and her paddle under the other, Dana burst out of the house and raced for the beach and Luke's kayak.

CHAPTER TEN

Bone-tired, Tyler fought the wind and waves on Badger Bay.

Having Jake slumped across the front of the kayak didn't help. The dog added seventy pounds to the front of the load that Tyler was trying to paddle to Crab Island.

Again and again, waves shoved them up in the air, then dropped them straight down into a trough.

Jake whined and shivered as he hugged the kayak with his front legs.

Maybe Tyler could have used deck line to tie the dog more securely to the boat. But he hadn't wanted to take a chance on losing his only paddle while he tried. And what if the boat flipped over? Jake wouldn't be able to get loose. He would drown.

So after every third or fourth stroke, Tyler grabbed Jake's collar and pulled the dog closer to the cockpit.

Tyler didn't know how long he'd been struggling across the bay when suddenly he heard a muffled roar.

A boat engine? Tyler's hopes soared. Was somebody coming to save them?

The next time a swell lifted them up, Tyler glanced quickly around. And his heart sank.

What he'd heard was definitely not a rescuer. It was the sound of giant waves smashing against the rocks of Crab Island.

For days all Tyler had thought about was getting to the island. Now he would have given anything to be so close to Parsons Point instead.

How could he land on Crab Island without crashing the kayak, himself, and Jake against those monster boulders?

Not that he had a choice. The waves swept toward shore, carrying the kayak along with them.

Tyler tried hopelessly to remember what he'd read in *Kayaking Basics* about landing in heavy surf. But his mind wasn't operating.

Soon he ran out of time. A powerful wave caught the purple kayak and thrust it toward the rocks.

That wave was met by a backwash from the island. The wall of water that piled up between the two buried the nose of the kayak, stopping it dead.

Jake tumbled off the bow and disappeared beneath the waters of Badger Bay. If Tyler hadn't been wedged into a tight cockpit, he would have been thrown out of the boat.

The next wave upended the kayak, forcing its nose down and its tail in the air. The boat slalomed along for a few yards before it flipped over completely.

Suddenly Tyler found himself upside down in the water. He was hanging under the kayak while an icy whirlpool spun him around and around.

Am I going to make it? he wondered, just before he turned loose his paddle and ripped open the spray skirt.

Tyler managed to kick himself free from the spinning boat.

He was freezing.

Tyler's life vest pushed him upward. His head broke the surface of the water just long enough for him to take a deep breath. Then another wave caught him and flung him closer to the rocks.

Tyler stuck his arms straight out from his sides, trying to slow himself down.

Something smooth and slick brushed against his right hand.

Giant jellyfish! he thought, jerking his hand away.

But the next time Tyler's head popped out of the water, he found himself eye to eye with Jake!

We'll go in together, Tyler told himself, grabbing Jake's collar.

Tyler looked over his shoulder, waiting until a wave was almost on top of them.

"Now or never," he said out loud. "GO, JAKE!" Tyler shouted to the dog.

Tyler kicked as hard as he could, and Jake paddled. They surfed forward on the crest of the wave.

Now they were so close to the island that Tyler could see greeny-brown seaweed waving on the rocks.

All at once the water was shallow. Through his wet suit, Tyler could feel his feet and knees scraping across stones scattered along a sandy bottom.

He struggled to stand up. But the next wave was already breaking, right on top of Tyler and the dog.

Tons of water came crashing down on the two of them.

The wave tore Tyler's hand away from Jake's collar.

66

It flung Tyler toward the huge gray rocks on the shoreline.

Tyler wrapped his arms around his head and pulled his legs in close to his body. He tumbled forward through bubbles and foam, thudding against one boulder and then another, like a runaway pinball.

There was a final crash. Tyler saw stars . . . then blackness for a moment. The wave pulled away from him, leaving him flat on his back . . . on land.

Tyler lay where he was for a second, staring up at the sky, until his head hurt a little less.

Then he struggled to sit up.

There was a huge gray rock to the left of him, another to the right, and an army of boulders behind those. Tyler had somehow landed on one of the few patches of sand around.

He'd been slapped down on the edge of Crab Island, with a killer bump above his left ear that was bleeding a little.

But he felt like the luckiest guy in the world. He was alive and not badly hurt.

Where was Jake?

"Jake! Jake!" Tyler shouted.

At first he didn't hear anything but the crashing of waves and his own teeth chattering with cold.

Then Tyler thought he heard a whine coming from somewhere to his right.

Shakily, he crawled onto a boulder and called again.

This time, Tyler got a bark for an answer.

"Keep it up, Jake!" Tyler yelled.

When he climbed over the next huge rock, he almost fell on top of a small, silvery seal.

It didn't look like any of the seals Tyler had seen at

Neptune. It had a black face, and the black marking across its back curved down its sides like wings.

When Tyler slid off the boulder, the seal struggled to pull itself away from him. That's when Tyler noticed that one of the seal's foreflippers had been sliced almost in half.

"Landing on Crab Island is hard on everybody," Tyler murmured.

Remembering Project Neptune rules, he didn't move any closer to the seal. "If I get off Crab Island, I promise I'll get you off, too," he whispered.

Then a couple of loud barks caught Tyler's attention.

He squeezed between several more boulders.

There was Jake, smiling up at him!

"You made it!" Tyler said to the dog, giving him a hug.

Jake's left ear was torn. He had a cut over his right eye, and he was holding up his right front foot. He yelped when Tyler touched it. And his skin was ice-cold. Tyler and the dog were both shivering so much that it was hard for either of them to stand up.

Tyler knew plenty about what cold could do to warm-blooded animals like Jake and him—such as kill them in no time. But he didn't know if he should take off his wet clothes—strip down to the wet suit—or if he should leave them on, since he didn't have anything dry to replace them with.

Tyler's head ached. He leaned back against a boulder . . . and the boulder was *warm*.

The dark gray rocks were soaking up heat from the sun, like natural solar collectors.

Tyler grabbed hold of Jake's collar and led the dog

even farther away from the salt spray, into a narrow space between a triangle of boulders.

Now he and the dog were protected from the wind and water, and the rocks could warm them a little.

Tyler took off the life vest, his jacket, and his wool shirt. He pulled off his sneakers and stepped out of his jeans. He laid the wet clothes across the top of a boulder, hoping they'd dry fast. Then he started stamping up and down to get the blood in his feet and legs moving.

Tyler figured he and Jake might be okay as long as there was daylight.

But what would happen when the sun sank lower in the sky and the air grew colder?

If someone didn't come for them before dark, Tyler knew they could freeze to death.

And he could think of an excellent reason why no one was likely to show up in time: He'd been so sneaky about what he was doing that morning that nobody had a clue where he was. And nobody would think he was crazy enough to try to paddle to Crab Island.

Jake wagged his tail. He was warming up, he had a friend with him, he felt safe. The dog laid his head on a toasty, flat stone and went to sleep.

An empty purple kayak might give someone an idea. But it could take as long as a day or two for the boat to wash ashore at Parsons Point. And maybe the current would push it straight out into the ocean instead.

Even if the Chapins somehow figured out that Tyler and Jake were marooned on Crab Island, how could they rescue them? The Mote twins said the island was surrounded by shallow sand bars—larger boats couldn't get close.

"I can't believe I was so dumb," Tyler said to Jake, who snored peacefully back at him.

CHAPTER ELEVEN

Dana was paddling Luke's yellow kayak furiously across Badger Bay, headed for Crab Island.

"I can't believe how dumb Tyler is!" she muttered as she stroked: right side, left side, right side. "He's supposed to know all about the Great Outdoors. Couldn't he even tell the weather was changing?"

The purple kayak was nowhere to be seen, so Dana didn't know if her dog and her cousin were still afloat, or if they'd been dumped into the pounding waves near the island—if they'd even made it that far.

Because of the strong wind and the currents, Dana wasn't traveling nearly as fast as she wanted to. Sticking the face of her paddle into the water, holding her elbows down low, she braced high to keep a big wave from tipping her over. She stared over the bow of the yellow kayak at the grim gray rocks strung out in front of her. "How's Tyler going to land?" she worried out loud. "How am *I* going to land?"

Luke had taught Dana how to hang back behind the breaking waves while she looked for a safe landing place. But Dana didn't know if there *was* a safe landing place on Crab Island.

Suddenly her heart skipped a beat: A slender purple hull tumbled end over end through the distant breakers.

"Where are they?" Dana murmured. Fearfully, she squinted at the water for signs of Tyler and Jake. But she couldn't pick out an orange life vest or her big yellow dog anywhere in the dark, churning sea.

"They must have made it onto the island," Dana told herself, and paddled even harder.

Huge waves tossed the yellow kayak upward, then left it hanging in midair to nosedive into the troughs between them. Dana couldn't see much more than sea spray, but she thought there might be an open space between the rocks at the north end of Crab.

Worn out and cold, Dana fought her way north against the current, keeping the kayak well beyond the line of breakers rolling toward the rocks. Finally she let herself be picked up by a giant wave. It carried the yellow kayak and Dana along as easily as a scrap of driftwood. Crab Island rapidly grew closer.

Before that wave could slam Dana onto the beach, she back-paddled into the smaller wave behind it. About ten yards from shore, Dana used a hard forward sweep to turn the yellow kayak around. She pointed the boat away from shore, as Luke had shown her, braced high against a third wave, and let it wash her all the way into the foam near the shoreline.

Still holding onto her paddle, Dana ripped the spray skirt from around her waist. She struggled out of the kayak into icy water above her knees.

A wave broke over Dana's head, almost snatching the kayak away from her. But she grabbed the handle at the tip of the bow and waded toward a sliver of sand, dragging the kayak along with her.

"I did it!" Dana gasped proudly. But she was too worried about Tyler and Jake to spend time patting herself on the back.

She pulled the yellow kayak as far away from the water as she could, up to the edges of the big rocks. She took off her blue life vest and reached into the boat's cockpit to check on the blankets. They were a lot drier than she was.

Then Dana climbed on top of the nearest boulder and peered anxiously around the island.

Crab Island was narrow and U-shaped, with the open part of the U facing the mainland. The island was almost flat, but it was crowded with gray rocks like the one Dana was standing on.

Which makes it hard to see anyone, especially if he's lying down, hurt, Dana thought. She'd just about decided that she'd have to check behind every boulder on Crab when she spotted a patch of orange on the far leg of the U. It was the exact color of a Neptune life vest.

Dana's heart jumped. An orange life vest would mean that Tyler had made it safely ashore, wouldn't it?

Dana slid off the rock and pulled the blankets out of Luke's kayak. She had to squeeze through, crawl over, or climb around what seemed like a hundred boulders, at least. She got scratched, scraped, and bruised, but the effort warmed her up.

She stopped every few minutes to shout, "Tyler! Jake! Where are you?" and to listen for an answer.

But the wind was howling now, and with the waves crashing on the shore, Dana couldn't have heard her cousin or Jake if they had answered her. She'd lost sight of the splash of orange, too. Dana was beginning to think she'd just imagined the color when she happened to glance down. Directly below her were the tips of a little seal's flippers—so still she was sure the animal was dead.

But as soon as Dana's feet touched the ground beside it, the little seal wedged itself farther under a rocky shelf, trying to hide.

"It's a harp seal," Dana murmured, recognizing the black marking across its back. She'd only seen two or three of them in her whole life: Harp seals were rare at Parsons Point.

Dana didn't move any nearer, but she did kneel down for a better look. The seal was thin, its fur was patchy, and a front flipper was badly cut. . . . All at once she noticed footprints in a pocket of sand—sneaker prints, and the outlines were sharp and fresh!

"Tyler's been here!" Dana exclaimed. She jumped to her feet to follow the trail of footprints: She lost it, found a few more prints next to a rock, squeezed between boulders . . . and practically stumbled over Tyler and Jake!

They were sleeping, looking as peaceful as if they'd been stretched out on the living-room couch at the lighthouse. Tyler was wearing a wet suit. His regular clothes and his sneakers were laid out on a rock to dry. He was using the orange life vest as a pillow. Jake's head rested on Tyler's knee.

Dana was so relieved to see them both that she was speechless for a moment.

"Tyler!" she yelled as soon as she got her breath back.

"Wh-what . . . ," Tyler stammered. He didn't seem to realize where he was for a split second.

And then he did. "Dana!" he said, a huge smile on his face.

Jake woke up, too. He struggled to his feet, whining happily at Dana.

"How did you find us?" Tyler said. "How did you know where I was? How did you get here? Where's Uncle Joe?"

"It wasn't easy, believe me!" Dana said, answering Tyler's next-to-last question first. She dropped a blanket over him. "Here."

"This feels great," Tyler said, wrapping the blanket around himself.

While Dana draped another blanket around her dog, she answered Tyler's second question: "I saw you from the lighthouse. I can't believe you did this, Tyler. Nobody ever kayaks to Crab Island, period. It's a miracle that you didn't drown!" She added to herself, *And that I didn't either.*

Dana went on, "If Laurie Miller hadn't seen you grab the life vest out of the barn, I wouldn't have had a clue you'd taken the kayak." She didn't bother to tell Tyler that she'd been certain he was running away to Alaska, and that she'd come back to the lighthouse to spy on him.

"I thought kayaking to Crab Island would make me famous at Rockport Middle School," Tyler admitted. "So Uncle Joe's here, too?" he asked hopefully.

Dana shook her head. "Mom and Dad are still in Bellvale," she said. "But I left a message on the blackboard near the stranding phone. They'll see it as soon as they get in."

74

"And Laurie Miller knows where you were going, right?" said Tyler.

"No time to tell her," said Dana. "Mom and Dad will come for us. Don't worry," she added, a lot more confidently than she felt.

I know the Coast Guard helicopter can't fly in strong wind, she was thinking. *And it couldn't land on Crab Island, anyway, not in the middle of all these rocks.*

Dana pulled the plastic bag of matches out of her pocket. "I'll gather some driftwood to start a fire," she said to her cousin. "It'll warm us up, and maybe the smoke will show Mom and Dad exactly where we are."

"Good idea," Tyler said, pulling on his sneakers to help her.

Tree limbs and branches that had washed onto Crab during past storms were wedged between the rocks. It didn't take Dana and Tyler long to gather armfuls of wood. It took them awhile to get a fire lit, though. Even in the sheltered space between boulders, wind swirled and gusted and blew out the matches.

But Tyler smashed some branches into kindling. Dana added a few scraps of paper that she'd found. And she and Tyler finally got a fire burning.

"Nice," Tyler said, moving close to the flames. "You don't have anything to eat, do you?"

Dana dug into her jacket pocket. She pulled out a hair clip, a rubber band . . . and a couple of old, sticky Mentos. She handed one to Tyler. Jake whined and licked his lips, so she stuck the other one in the dog's mouth.

"Now what do we do?" Tyler said.

"We wait until they get here," said Dana. She crossed her fingers under the third blanket.

75

"Did you see the little seal?" Tyler asked suddenly.
Dana nodded. "We'll save it, too."
"Hey, Dana," Tyler said quietly.
"Yeah?" said Dana, almost too tired to speak.
"Thanks for coming after me," Tyler said.

CHAPTER TWELVE

Tyler, Dana, and Jake were huddled together near the fire, under all three of the blankets, as the sun sank toward the mainland. Tyler had put his clothes back on over the wet suit, but he was still cold. He could feel Dana and Jake shivering, too.

"I wonder if it's dropped below freezing yet," Tyler said. Could they make it through a frosty night on Crab Island?

Then he asked his cousin for the third or fourth time, "How long do Uncle Joe and Aunt Lissa usually stay in Bellvale at the hardware store?"

"I told you—it depends on what they need to buy," Dana answered, "and whether or not they have lunch at Barth's Luncheonette, or get fast food instead, and if—"

"What do you like to eat at Barth's Luncheonette?" Tyler interrupted. He thought about burgers and fries, and his stomach started growling.

"Tyler, this doesn't help at all," Dana said.

"It's too bad you didn't tell somebody before you left the Point," Tyler mumbled—he couldn't stop himself.

"And it's too bad you didn't stay at the lighthouse where you belonged," Dana said crossly, "instead of 'exploring' Crab Island. I didn't take the time to tell anybody because I thought you might be drowning!"

Suddenly there was a flash of white light over their heads.

"Wow! What was that?" Tyler exclaimed. He dropped his side of the blankets and jumped to his feet.

Dana stood up, too, and Jake barked a couple of times—he'd seen the flash as well.

"Maybe some kind of weird ocean lightning?" Tyler said uneasily. A serious storm was the last thing they needed on Crab.

But Dana said, "Uh-uh—no thunder."

Tyler pulled himself onto the nearest boulder. Dana was right behind him.

"It couldn't have been the light at the Coast Guard station," Dana said. "That would come from a different direction."

A second flash caught Tyler full in the face. "I can't see anything now!" he said.

"I can't believe it!" Dana exclaimed.

"What? What?" Tyler said. He rubbed his eyes hard, trying to clear away the black spots.

"It's the beacon at our lighthouse!" said Dana. "This is the first time I've ever seen it shine. I think Mom and Dad are letting us know that they're coming for us."

Tyler could see again: A brilliant white light was slowly sweeping across the island from one end to the other.

But the sun had almost set. And it wasn't possible to land on Crab Island in a large boat even in the daytime.

"How can they get close enough to pick us up?" Tyler asked his cousin.

"They'll think of a way," Dana said, although she didn't sound very convincing. "In the meantime, let's try to keep warm."

Tyler and Dana slid down off the rock. They added more driftwood to their fire and covered themselves, and Jake, with the blankets again.

Night fell on the island. It was *dark*—no moon, no stars, nothing except their sputtering fire.

Tyler and Dana dozed.

Jake's whining startled them awake.

"I think he hears something," Dana said to Tyler.

Tyler listened: The crashing of the waves muffled any other sounds.

But wasn't that a pounding noise? Like some kind of . . .

"Diesel engines!" Dana said. The cousins scrambled onto the rock again.

"It's the *Sea Spirit,* Captain Sokel's boat!" said Dana.

Lights shone in the wheelhouse of a big white boat. A searchlight on the front of it was pointed squarely at the island.

Dana jumped off the rock to grab a dry branch. She stuck it into the fire until it blazed. Then she handed it to Tyler: "Here—hold it high!"

The branch burned just long enough for the searchlight to catch Tyler in its beam.

"They see us!" Tyler yelled, jumping up and down.

After that, things moved quickly.

Captain Sokel maneuvered the *Sea Spirit* as close to Crab Island as he could without getting stuck on a sand

79

bar. A voice called out on a bullhorn: "Dana, it's Dad! We're shooting a line to you. Pull on it until you've got some rope in your hand. Then tie the rope to a rock—*tight*!"

The searchlight swung sideways to shine on some boulders a safe distance away from the kids. In a minute or two there was a loud bang from the boat. An iron bar flew through the air and clattered against the rocks. It carried yards and yards of nylon cord along with it from the *Sea Spirit* to the island.

Dana and Tyler pulled on the cord until their arms ached and they were out of breath.

"Wh-why are we doing this, exactly?" Tyler huffed.

"We're working our way to the heavier rope," Dana told him. "We'll tie that rope to a boulder, and Dad'll use it to guide himself over here in a raft."

Tyler knotted the guide rope to a huge rock. Then Uncle Joe and another guy lashed a big inflatable raft to the far end of it. Tyler and Dana could see them in the spotlight's beam. The raft pitched through the waves, right up to the island.

Uncle Joe leaped out of the raft even before it bumped ashore, leaving the second guy aboard, and Dana ran into his arms. "Oh, Dad, am I glad to see you!" she said, starting to cry.

Tyler didn't really trust his own voice, either.

Uncle Joe gave Tyler a big hug. "You're both safe! And Jake, too," he added, as the yellow dog barked excitedly.

Uncle Joe went on, "But what were you two thinking of? You could so easily have drowned, or been killed on the rocks, or frozen to death . . ."

"It's all my fault," Tyler said quickly. "I paddled

off in Dana's kayak by myself. I didn't know Jake had followed me until it was too late to take him back. And I had some problems with wind. And waves. And currents . . ."

The other guy had pulled the rubber raft onto the beach, away from the water.

"It's Luke!" said Dana.

"You did good," Luke said to her, swinging Dana around. "But I think you could stand a few more lessons," he told Tyler.

"I think kayaks are off-limits indefinitely," said Uncle Joe. "But we'll talk about that later. Your Aunt Lissa's out there on the boat. She's sent over a thermos of hot chocolate, and chicken sandwiches, and carrot cake. . . ."

"Even dog biscuits, just in case," Luke stuck in, "and we have lanterns, sleeping bags for everybody, a tarp to make a shelter, a medicine kit, and dry clothes for both of you—a bunch of stuff."

"Sleeping bags?" said Dana. "We're staying here?"

"Just for tonight," said her dad. "It'll be a lot safer to leave the island in the morning, when we can see what we're doing."

So I can tell Charlie and Carter that I spent the night on Crab Island! Tyler thought. *Totally cool!*

"Now, how about some dinner?" Luke said, unwrapping a chicken sandwich. "You guys have to be starving!"

"Uh . . . before I eat, there's something I'd like to show Uncle Joe," Tyler said.

"What's that?" said Mr. Chapin.

"A stranded seal for Neptune," said Tyler.

"You'll never find it in the dark," Dana said.

"We can't do anything for it until tomorrow, Tyler," his uncle told him. "The cold won't affect it; seals have a layer of blubber to keep them warm. And we'd frighten it to death with our flashlights."

"First thing in the morning, then," Tyler said.

He hoped the little harp seal could make it through the night.

 **CHAPTER THIRTEEN**

When Tyler woke up the next morning, the sun was just rising above the rocks around the shelter. Every one of his muscles ached—he felt as though he'd run in a marathon. Tyler snuggled farther into his down sleeping bag, but just for a moment: Dana was still asleep a few feet away, but Uncle Joe was already building a fire, with Jake keeping him company, and Luke was gathering more driftwood.

And Tyler remembered the harp seal.

He scrambled out of the sleeping bag, pulled on his sneakers and his jacket, and joined Uncle Joe and Jake at the fire.

"You don't look too bad," said his uncle, peering closely at Tyler. "A few scratches, and you've got a major bruise on the side of your head. But I'd say you were fairly lucky, wouldn't you?"

"Definitely," Tyler said.

"Tyler, your dad left you in our care," Uncle Joe went on. "What if something terrible had happened to you out here? How would your aunt and I have felt?

How could I have ever explained it to Jim? This escapade could have ended your life, and Dana's, and ruined your father's, mine, and your aunt's as well."

Tyler hadn't thought of it that way when he'd started paddling toward Crab Island; he'd just thought about impressing the kids at Rockport Middle School. But now he nodded. "I'm really sorry, Uncle Joe," he said. "It won't ever happen again."

"No, it can't," said his uncle. "And you'll be grounded for a month. You can leave the Point only to go to school and back, unless you're with your aunt or me."

"Okay," Tyler said.

"If Dana's kayak doesn't wash up somewhere in fairly good shape, we'll think of a way for you to earn some money to buy her a new one," Uncle Joe went on.

Dana surprised Tyler by mumbling sleepily from behind him, "I'll help."

"Good morning, sweetie," said Uncle Joe. "Why don't you two have a cookie for breakfast, and then we'll all look for that stranded seal Tyler was talking about."

The little harp seal was wedged under the same rock. It was still alive, although its breathing was shallow. Uncle Joe and Luke carefully eased the seal out. They wrapped it in one of the blankets and carried it to the beach where the rubber raft was waiting.

"We'll get you kids and Jake back to the *Sea Spirit* first," Uncle Joe said in a low voice to Tyler and Dana. "Then Luke and I will pack everything up here and bring the harp seal with us."

"I'd rather wait and go over with the seal," Tyler whispered, "if that's okay."

"That's okay," said his uncle.

Tyler watched him and Luke maneuver the rubber raft through the swells and over to the *Sea Spirit* with Dana and Jake aboard. Aunt Lissa was waiting by the railing to give Dana a huge hug the second her daughter set foot on deck.

Then Uncle Joe and Luke brought the raft back down the safety line to pick up Tyler and the harp seal.

"Have you thought of a good name for this guy?" Luke murmured to Tyler when they laid the seal on a bed of blankets in the raft.

"What about Lucky?" Tyler whispered back.

"I think that would be a good name for both of you," said Uncle Joe.

As the four of them headed across the bay toward the boat, Tyler hardly took his eyes off Lucky. But he did glance up once to see Dana smiling at him over the railing of the *Sea Spirit,* giving him a thumbs-up.

Tyler wasn't sure if his cousin meant it for him, or for the little harp seal. But he returned it with both hands.

AFTERWORD

In the summertime I live on the East End of Long Island, New York, a mile or so from the Atlantic Ocean. But my real introduction to marine mammals in the wild was a whale-watching cruise I took several years ago, off Brier Island in Nova Scotia, Canada. That day I saw at least a dozen humpbacks, some of them almost close enough to touch, and it was one of the most exciting experiences of my life.

Whale-watching cruises are just one of the ways that groups involved in rescuing sick or injured marine mammals and sea turtles raise money to continue their work. The Riverhead Foundation for Marine Research and Preservation, not far from my house, also sponsors seal-watching cruises. It offers memberships in its organization, and "adoption" programs to provide food and medicine for rescued animals. For a small donation, the adopter receives a story and photographs of an animal actually recovering at the Foundation, and a phone number to call to check on its progress.

Marine-mammal rescue groups like The Riverhead

Foundation rely on volunteers of all ages, just as Project Neptune does, to find stranded animals and care for them, as well as to help in the office, prepare newsletters and bulletins, and join the whale- and seal-watching cruises as guides.

Through their work, these organizations hope to undo even a little of the damage that humankind has done to the marine environment. If you'd like to learn more about them, here are the mailing addresses, telephone numbers, and Web addresses for just a few:

The Riverhead Foundation for Marine Research and Preservation
431 East Main Street
Riverhead, NY 11901
Telephone: (516) 369-9840
FAX: (516) 369-9826
http://www.riverheadfoundation.org

The Marine Mammal Stranding Center of New Jersey
P.O. Box 773
Brigantine, NJ 08203
Telephone: (609) 266-0538
http://www.mmsc.org

The Marine Mammal Center (Northern California)
Telephone: (415) 289-SEAL
http://www.tmmc.org

Texas Marine Mammal Stranding Network
4700 Avenue U, Bldg. 303
Galveston, TX 77551
http://www.tmmsn.org

Nova Scotia Stranding Network
c/o Nova Scotia Museum
1747 Summer Street
Halifax, NS B3H3A6 Canada
Telephone: (902) 494-3723
http://is.dal.ca/~whitelab/strand.htm